A. A. MILNE

Kanga and Baby Roo Come to the Forest

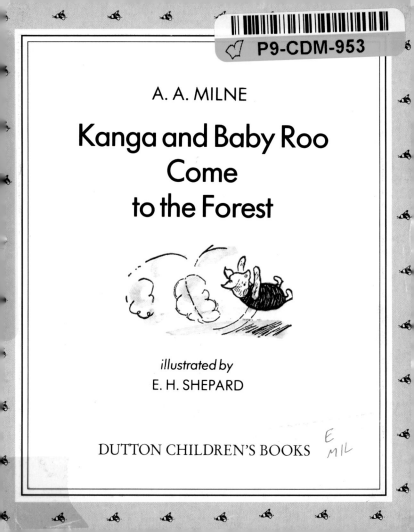

illustrated by
E. H. SHEPARD

DUTTON CHILDREN'S BOOKS

E
MIL

Kanga and Baby Roo
Come to the Forest

Nobody seemed to know where they came from, but there they were in the Forest: Kanga and Baby Roo. When Pooh asked Christopher Robin, 'How did they come here?'

Christopher Robin said, 'In the Usual Way, if you know what I mean, Pooh,' and Pooh, who didn't, said 'Oh!' Then he nodded his head twice and said, 'In the Usual Way. Ah!'

Then he went to call upon his friend Piglet to see what *he* thought about it. And at Piglet's house he found Rabbit. So they all talked about it together.

'What I don't like about it is this,' said Rabbit. 'Here are we – you, Pooh, and you, Piglet, and Me – and suddenly—'

'And Eeyore,' said Pooh.

'And Eeyore – and then suddenly—'

'And Owl,' said Pooh.

'And Owl – and then all of a sudden—'

'Oh, and Eeyore,' said Pooh. 'I was forgetting *him*.'

'Here – we – are,' said Rabbit very slowly and carefully, 'all – of – us, and then, suddenly, we wake up one morning, and what do we find? We find a Strange Animal among us. An animal of whom we had never even heard before! An animal who carries her family about with her in her pocket! Suppose *I* carried *my* family about with me in *my* pocket, how many pockets should I want?'

'Sixteen,' said Piglet.

'Seventeen, isn't it?' said Rabbit. 'And one more for a handkerchief – that's eighteen. Eighteen pockets in one suit! I haven't time.'

There was a long and thoughtful silence . . . and then Pooh, who had been frowning very hard for some minutes, said: '*I* make it fifteen.'

'What?' said Rabbit.

'Fifteen.'

'Fifteen what?'

'Your family.'

'What about them?'

Pooh rubbed his nose and said that he thought Rabbit had been talking about his family.

'Did I?' said Rabbit carelessly.

'Yes, you said—'

'Never mind, Pooh,' said Piglet impatiently. 'The question is, What are we to do about Kanga?'

'Oh, I see,' said Pooh.

'The best way,' said Rabbit, 'would be this. The best way would be to steal Baby Roo and hide him, and then when Kanga says, "Where's Baby Roo?" we say, "*Aha!*"'

'*Aha!*' said Pooh, practising. '*Aha! Aha!* . . . Of course,' he went on, 'we could say "Aha!" even if we hadn't stolen Baby Roo.'

'Pooh,' said Rabbit kindly, 'you haven't any brain.

'I know,' said Pooh humbly.

'We say "*Aha!*" so that Kanga knows that *we* know where Baby Roo is. "*Aha!*" means

"We'll tell you where Baby Roo is, if
you promise to go away from the Forest
and never come back." Now don't talk while
I think.'

Pooh went into a corner and tried saying
'Aha!' in that sort of voice. Sometimes it
seemed to him that it did mean what Rabbit
said, and sometimes it seemed to him that it
didn't. 'I suppose it's just practice,' he
thought. 'I wonder if Kanga will have to
practise too so as to understand it.'

'There's just one thing,' said Piglet,
fidgeting a bit. 'I was talking to Christopher
Robin, and he said that a Kanga was Generally
Regarded as One of the Fiercer Animals. I
am not frightened of Fierce Animals in the
ordinary way, but it is well known that if
One of the Fiercer Animals is Deprived of Its
Young, it becomes as fierce as Two of the
Fiercer Animals. In which case "*Aha!*" is
perhaps a *foolish* thing to say.'

'Piglet,' said Rabbit, taking out a pencil,

and licking the end of it, 'you haven't any pluck.'

'It is hard to be brave,' said Piglet, sniffing slightly, 'when you're only a Very Small Animal.'

Rabbit, who had begun to write very busily, looked up and said: 'It is because you are a very small animal that you will be Useful in the adventure before us.'

Piglet was so excited at the idea of being Useful that he forgot to be frightened any more, and when Rabbit went on to say that Kangas were only Fierce during the winter months, being at other times of an Affectionate Disposition, he could hardly sit still, he was so eager to begin being useful at once.

'What about me?' said Pooh sadly. 'I suppose *I* shan't be useful?'

'Never mind, Pooh,' said Piglet comfortingly. 'Another time perhaps.'

'Without Pooh,' said Rabbit solemnly as he sharpened his pencil, 'the adventure would be impossible.'

'Oh!' said Piglet, and tried not to look disappointed.

But Pooh went into a corner of the room and said proudly to himself,

'Impossible without Me! *That* sort of Bear.'

'Now listen all of you,' said Rabbit when he had finished writing, and Pooh and Piglet sat listening very eagerly with their mouths open. This was what Rabbit read out:

PLAN TO CAPTURE BABY ROO

1. *General Remarks.* Kanga runs faster than any of Us, even Me.
2. *More General Remarks.* Kanga never takes her eyes off Baby Roo, except when he's safely buttoned up in her pocket.

3. *Therefore*. If we are to capture Baby Roo, we must get a Long Start, because Kanga runs faster than any of Us, even Me. (*See* 1.)

4. *A Thought*. If Roo had jumped out of Kanga's pocket and Piglet had jumped in, Kanga wouldn't know the difference, because Piglet is a Very Small Animal.

5. Like Roo.

6. But Kanga would have to be looking the other way first, so as not to see Piglet jumping in.

7. See 2.

8. *Another Thought*. But if Pooh was talking to her very excitedly, she *might* look the other way for a moment.

9. And then I could run away with Roo.

10. Quickly.

11. *And Kanga wouldn't discover the difference until Afterwards.*

Well, Rabbit read this out proudly, and
for a little while after he had read it nobody
said anything. And then Piglet, who had been
opening and shutting his mouth without
making any noise, managed to say very
huskily:

'And – Afterwards?'

'How do you mean?'

'When Kanga *does* Discover the Difference?'

'Then we all say "*Aha!*"'

'All three of us?'

'Yes.'

'Oh!'

'Why, what's the trouble, Piglet?'

'Nothing,' said Piglet, 'as long as *we all
three* say it. As long as we all three say it,'
said Piglet, 'I don't mind,' he said, 'but I
shouldn't care to say "*Aha!*" by myself.
It wouldn't sound *nearly* so well. By the way,'
he said, 'you *are* quite sure about what you said
about the winter months?'

'The winter months?'

'Yes, only being Fierce in the Winter Months.'

'Oh, yes, yes, that's all right. Well, Pooh? You see what you have to do?'

'No,' said Pooh Bear. 'Not yet,' he said. 'What *do* I do?'

'Well, you just have to talk very hard to Kanga so as she doesn't notice anything.'

'Oh! What about?'

'Anything you like.'

'You mean like telling her a little bit of poetry or something?'

'That's it,' said Rabbit. 'Splendid. Now come along.'

So they all went out to look for Kanga.

Kanga and Roo were spending a quiet afternoon in a sandy part of the Forest. Baby Roo was practising very small jumps in the sand, and falling down mouse-holes and climbing out of them, and Kanga was fidgeting about and saying 'Just one more jump, dear, and then we must go home.' And at that moment who should come stumping up the hill but Pooh.

'Good afternoon, Kanga.'

'Good afternoon, Pooh.'

'Look at me jumping,' squeaked Roo, and fell into another mouse-hole.

'Hallo, Roo, my little fellow!'

'We were just going home,' said Kanga. 'Good afternoon, Rabbit. Good afternoon, Piglet.'

Rabbit and Piglet, who had now come up from the other side of the hill, said 'Good afternoon,' and 'Hallo, Roo,' and Roo asked them to look at him jumping, so they stayed and looked.

And Kanga looked too. . . .

'Oh, Kanga,' said Pooh, after Rabbit had winked at him twice, 'I don't know if you are interested in Poetry at all?'

'Hardly at all,' said Kanga.

'Oh!' said Pooh.

'Roo, dear, just one more jump and then
we must go home.'

There was a short silence while Roo fell
down another mouse-hole.

'Go on,' said Rabbit in a loud whisper
behind his paw.

'Talking of Poetry,' said Pooh, 'I made up
a little piece as I was coming along. It went like
this. Er – now let me see—'

'Fancy!' said Kanga. 'Now Roo, dear—'

'You'll like this piece of poetry,' said Rabbit.

'You'll love it,' said Piglet.

'You must listen very carefully,' said Rabbit.

'So as not to miss any of it,' said Piglet.

'Oh, yes,' said Kanga, but she still looked at Baby Roo.

'*How* did it go, Pooh?' said Rabbit.

Pooh gave a little cough and began.

LINES WRITTEN BY
A BEAR OF VERY LITTLE BRAIN

On Monday, when the sun is hot
I wonder to myself a lot:
'Now is it true, or is it not,
'That what is which and which is what?'

On Tuesday, when it hails and snows,
The feeling on me grows and grows
That hardly anybody knows
If those are these or these are those.

On Wednesday, when the sky is blue,
And I have nothing else to do,
I sometimes wonder if it's true
That who is what and what is who.

On Thursday, when it starts to freeze
And hoar-frost twinkles on the trees,
How very readily one sees
That these are whose – but whose are these?

On Friday—

'Yes, it is, isn't it?' said Kanga, not waiting to hear what happened on Friday. 'Just one more jump, Roo, dear, and then we really *must* be going.'

Rabbit gave Pooh a hurrying-up sort of nudge.

'Talking of Poetry,' said Pooh quickly, 'have you ever noticed that tree right over there?'

'Where?' said Kanga. 'Now, Roo—'

'Right over there,' said Pooh, pointing behind Kanga's back.

'No,' said Kanga. 'Now jump in, Roo, dear, and we'll go home.'

'You ought to look at that tree right over there,' said Rabbit. 'Shall I lift you in, Roo?' And he picked up Roo in his paws.

'I can see a bird in it from here,' said Pooh. 'Or is it a fish?'

'You ought to see that bird from here,' said Rabbit. 'Unless it's a fish.'

'It isn't a fish, it's a bird,' said Piglet.

'So it is,' said Rabbit.

'Is it a starling or a blackbird?' said Pooh.

'That's the whole question,' said Rabbit. 'Is it a blackbird or a starling?'

And then at last Kanga did turn her head to look. And the moment that her head was turned, Rabbit said in a loud voice 'In you go, Roo!' and in jumped Piglet into Kanga's pocket, and off scampered Rabbit, with Roo in his paws, as fast as he could.

'Why, where's Rabbit?' said Kanga, turning round again. 'Are you all right, Roo, dear?'

Piglet made a squeaky Roo-noise from the bottom of Kanga's pocket.

'Rabbit had to go away,' said Pooh. 'I think he thought of something he had to go and see about suddenly.'

'And Piglet?'

'I think Piglet thought of something at the same time. Suddenly.'

'Well, we must be getting home,' said

Kanga. 'Good-bye, Pooh.' And in three large jumps she was gone.

Pooh looked after her as she went.

'I wish I could jump like that,' he thought. 'Some can and some can't. That's how it is.'

But there were moments when Piglet wished that Kanga couldn't. Often, when he had had a long walk home through the Forest, he had wished that he were a bird; but now he thought jerkily to himself at the bottom of Kanga's pocket,

```
        this                        take
   'If      is      shall      really      to
            flying I        never              it.'
```

And as he went up in the air he said, '*Ooooooo!*'
and as he came down he said, '*Ow!*' And he
was saying, '*Ooooooo-ow, Ooooooo-ow,*
Ooooooo-ow' all the way to Kanga's house.

Of course as soon as Kanga unbuttoned
her pocket, she saw what had happened. Just
for a moment, she thought she was frightened,
and then she knew she wasn't; for she felt
sure that Christopher Robin would never let
any harm happen to Roo. So she said to her-
self, 'If they are having a joke with me,
I will have a joke with them.'

'Now then, Roo, dear,' she said as she
took Piglet out of her pocket. 'Bed-time.'

'*Aha!*' said Piglet, as well as he could
after his Terrifying Journey. But it wasn't

a very good '*Aha!*' and Kanga didn't seem
to understand what it meant.

'Bath first,' said Kanga in a cheerful
voice.

'*Aha!*' said Piglet again, looking anxiously
for the others. But the others weren't there.
Rabbit was playing with Baby Roo in his own
house, and feeling more fond of him every
minute, and Pooh, who had decided to be
a Kanga, was still at the sandy place on the top
of the Forest, practising jumps.

'I am not at all sure,' said Kanga in a
thoughtful voice, 'that it wouldn't be
a good idea to have a *cold* bath this
evening. Would you like that, Roo, dear?'

Piglet, who had never been really fond
of baths, shuddered a long indignant
shudder, and said in as brave a voice as
he could: 'Kanga, I see that the time has
come to speak plainly.'

'Funny little Roo,' said Kanga, as she
got the bath-water ready.

'I am *not* Roo,' said Piglet loudly. 'I
am Piglet!'

'Yes, dear, yes,' said Kanga soothingly.
'And imitating Piglet's voice too! So
clever of him,' she went on, as she took

a large bar of yellow soap out of the cupboard. 'What *will* he be doing next?'

'Can't you *see*?' shouted Piglet. 'Haven't you got *eyes*? *Look* at me!'

'I *am* looking, Roo, dear,' said Kanga rather severely. 'And you know what I told you yesterday about making faces. If you go on making faces like Piglet's you will grow up to *look* like Piglet – and *then* think how sorry you will be. Now then, into the

bath, and don't let me have to speak to you
about it again.'

Before he knew where he was, Piglet was
in the bath, and Kanga was scrubbing him
firmly with a large lathery flannel.

'*Ow!*' cried Piglet. 'Let me out! I'm Piglet!'

'Don't open the mouth, dear, or the soap
goes in,' said Kanga. 'There! What did I tell
you?'

'You – you – you did it on purpose,'
spluttered Piglet, as soon as he could speak
again . . . and then accidentally had another
mouthful of lathery flannel.

'That's right, dear, don't say anything,' said
Kanga, and in another minute Piglet was
out of the bath, and being rubbed dry
with a towel.

'Now,' said Kanga, 'there's your medicine,
and then bed.'

'W-w-what medicine?' said Piglet.

'To make you grow big and strong, dear.
You don't want to grow up small and weak

like Piglet, do you? Well, then!'

At that moment there was a knock at the door.

'Come in,' said Kanga, and in came Christopher Robin.

'Christopher Robin, Christopher Robin!' cried Piglet. 'Tell Kanga who I am! She keeps saying I'm Roo. I'm not Roo, am I!'

Christopher Robin looked at him very carefully, and shook his head.

'You can't be Roo,' he said, 'because I've just seen Roo playing in Rabbit's house.'

'Well!' said Kanga. 'Fancy that! Fancy my making a mistake like that.'

'There you are!' said Piglet. 'I told you so. I'm Piglet.'

Christopher Robin shook his head again.

'Oh, you're not Piglet,' he said. 'I know Piglet well, and he's *quite* a different colour.'

Piglet began to say that this was because he had just had a bath, and then he thought that perhaps he wouldn't say that, and as he opened his mouth to say something else, Kanga slipped the medicine spoon in, and then patted him on the back and told him that it was really quite a nice taste when you got used to it.

'I knew it wasn't Piglet,' said Kanga. 'I wonder who it can be.'

'Perhaps it's some relation of Pooh's,' said Christopher Robin. 'What about a nephew or an uncle or something?'

Kanga agreed that this was probably what it was, and said that they would have to call it by some name.

'I shall call it Pootel,' said Christopher Robin. 'Henry Pootel for short.'

And just when it was decided, Henry Pootel wriggled out of Kanga's arms and jumped to the ground. To his great joy Christopher Robin had left the door open. Never had Henry Pootel Piglet run so fast as he ran then, and he didn't stop running until he had got quite close to his house. But when he was a hundred yards away he stopped running, and rolled the rest of the way home, so as to get his own nice comfortable colour again. . . .

So Kanga and Roo stayed in the Forest. And every Tuesday Roo spent the day with his great friend Rabbit, and every Tuesday Kanga spent the day with her great friend Pooh, teaching him to jump, and every Tuesday Piglet spent the day with his great friend Christopher Robin. So they were all happy again.